Adopting a Dinosaur
Somos8 Series

© Text: José Carlos Andrés, 2018
© Illustrations: Ana Sanfelippo, 2018
© Edition: NubeOcho, 2019
www.nubeocho.com · hello@nubeocho.com

Original title: *Adoptar un dinosaurio*
English translation: Ben Dawlatly
Text editing: Rebecca Packard

Distributed in the United States by
Consortium Book Sales & Distribution

First edition: 2019
ISBN: 978-84-17123-63-5

Printed in China by Asia Pacific Offset,
respecting international labor standards.

ADOPTING A DINOSAUR

José Carlos Andrés   Ana Sanfelippo

nubeOCHO

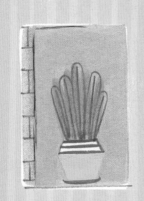

TUESDAY

I WANT A CAT,
I WANT A CAT,
IWANNACAT.

WEDNESDAY

I WANT A TURTLE,
I WANT A TURTLE,
IWANNATURTLE.

But Ali's parents
would always answer:

ANIMALS AT HOME? NOOO WAY!!

On her way home from school, Ali found an enormous egg in the park. Since it looked abandoned, she decided to take it back to her house.

She tried to hide it, but it didn't fit anywhere.

TUESDAY

WEDNESDAY

Ali called the egg Kimo. She painted two eyes and a red nose on him and added a mop for hair.

She polished Kimo and lit a lamp beside him so that he would stay warm.

In the evening, she covered him
with a blanket and told him a story.

The egg hatched.

CRACK!
CRAACK!!
CRAACK!!!

A few seconds later a big
head appeared and said,

ROARRR!!

Ali's parents thought that was impossible, so they answered:

"Okay, if you find one, we'll adopt it."

"Dad, Mom, this is Kimo."

Ali came out of her
room hugging a
baby saltasaurus.

After the initial shock wore off, it turned out
that Kimo was very sweet.

But not for everyone, because in the park
he frightened a few people!

Kimo, Ali and the other kids
played together and had loads of fun.

Suddenly, the earth began to shake, and Kimo heard a familiar sound. He pricked his ears, scratched his back on a tree and roared with a smile.

At that moment, two huge saltasauruses appeared. When they saw their little baby, they began to lick him, and they huddled together.

Kimo left with his parents, but first, he said goodbye to Ali and her family.

The house seemed very empty
when Kimo left.

"Why don't we adopt a dog, a cat,
a turtle or a parrot?"
"Or a chicken, a pig,
a giraffe or an elephant?!"

Ali missed Kimo so much,
but she didn't want another animal...

...because from time to time,
they would have a visit, a very special visit.